Far Enough Island

by Lesley Choyce

illustrated by Jill Quinn

Pottersfield Press
Lawrencetown Beach
Nova Scotia, Canada

Canadian Cataloguing in Publication Data

Choyce, Lesley
    Far enough island
    (Children's chapter books)
    ISBN 10895900-33-6
I. Quinn, Jill.   II. Title.   III. Series.
PS8555.H668F37 2000   jC813'.54   C00-950126-6
PZ7.C448Fa 2000

Edited by Carol McDougall

Pottersfield Press gratefully acknowledges the ongoing support of the Nova Scotia Department of Tourism and Culture, Cultural Affairs Division as well as The Canada Council for the Arts. We acknowledge the financial support of the Government of Canada through the Book Publishing Industry Development Program for our publishing activities.

Pottersfield Press
83 Leslie Road
East Lawrencetown
Nova Scotia, Canada, B2Z 1P8
To order, phone toll-free 1-800-NIMBUS9
1-800-646-2879

Printed in Canada

THE CANADA COUNCIL | LE CONSEIL DES ARTS
FOR THE ARTS | DU CANADA
SINCE 1957 | DEPUIS 1957

Canadä

NOVA SCOTIA
Tourism and Culture

Chapter One

Sarah MacNeil wished that her mother could be happier. But there was nothing she seemed to be able to do about it. Sarah was afraid her mother was the unhappiest mother in the whole world. Yet, when Sarah woke up on a sunny summer morning in Nova Scotia, she found it hard to believe that anyone could be unhappy here.

Her bedroom looked out over a blue sparkling inlet. Sea gulls swooped up and down and a great blue heron

walked gingerly through the shallows.
Off toward the ocean, she could see the
outline of Far Enough Island. Sarah
thought that there was something
magical about Far Enough Island.
Nobody lived on the island and she had
never set foot on it. It was always just
there in her bedroom window, full of
interesting possibilities.

Jeremiah was scratching at her door.
Good old Jeremiah. He was her crazy,
wonderful dog and the best friend she
ever had.

"Sarah, get up and let your dog
outside!" her mother yelled from the
kitchen.

Sarah jumped up from bed and let
Jeremiah into her room. Jeremiah dove
at her and knocked her down on the
floor, licking her nose and slobbering all
over her face.

"What's going on up there?" her
mother yelled again.

"Nothing," Sarah answered. She loved Jeremiah more than anything in the world. "Dad didn't let you go with him on the boat again today, did he?" she said to her dog.

Jeremiah just rolled over on the floor and scratched himself by wiggling back and forth, upside down on the floor.

Sarah changed into her clothes in seconds and ran outside with Jeremiah right on her heels. She raced at top speed to the end of the wharf, stopping at the very last second before toppling over into the icy water. Jeremiah galloped along behind her but didn't stop at the end of the wharf. He just kept running straight out over the end, his feet kicking at the empty air. Then he splashed down hard into the water, surfaced, and turned around to swim back to shore.

Sarah laughed and laughed. It was one of the games she liked to play with

Jeremiah in the summer. He probably could have stopped if he wanted to, but Sarah knew he was a good swimmer and Jeremiah always seemed so happy after being tricked into flying off the end of the wharf. Now he was on the shoreline, shaking himself, a million water drops flying in all directions.

Out past Far Enough Island, Sarah could see her dad's boat coming back from sea. That seemed strange. He never came in this early in the day.

Sarah walked back to the house and went into the kitchen where her mother was worrying over a pile of papers at the table. Jeremiah bounded past her and shook himself in the middle of the kitchen floor.

Sarah's mother went off like a canon. "Get that wet beast out of here!"

"Sorry. I'll clean it up," Sarah said. The last thing she needed was to get her mother mad. Sarah reached for a towel and began to mop the water drops off of everything, including her mother. She grabbed poor Jeremiah by the collar and skidded him across the floor and back out the door. Jeremiah looked very unhappy about being thrown out.

"Why is Daddy headed back in so soon?" Sarah asked her mother. She was used to her father's boat arriving back from fishing at around eleven or twelve o'clock. She saw that it was only nine-thirty.

"The fish are almost all gone. There are hardly any left," Sarah's mother said, her voice like dry gravel.

"But there must be millions of fish in the sea."

"Well, not around here, there's not. Get yourself some cereal for breakfast."

"Sure." Sarah filled a bowl to the very top.

"Sarah, that's too much. Don't waste it. Money doesn't grow on trees, you know."

Sarah poured half of it back into the box. Why didn't money grow on trees? she wondered. In fact, it should. Her parents were always worrying about money and Sarah couldn't see why. They weren't exactly poor.

Jeremiah had managed to stand on his two legs at the door and turn the doorknob with his paw. He had it open a crack, just enough so that he could stick his nose through. He looked so funny that Sarah thought she was going to burst out laughing and spit her cereal all over the floor. Instead, she held it in, but she couldn't help having a big funny lopsided grin on her face as she tried to chew.

Her mother looked up at her. She was very upset about something. But it couldn't be Sarah. Sarah was just being herself.

"Why are you smiling like that?"

Sarah shrugged her shoulders.

"Well, never smile without a good reason. You should know that. People will think there's something wrong with you. Never smile before Christmas. That's what my mother used to say." She let a out a deep sigh. "And even then there's not always anything to smile about."

Chapter Two

Jeremiah had arrived in the middle of the night, three years before. It was during the worst hurricane Nova Scotia had seen in fifty years.

"What is that?" little Sarah asked. She had heard a strange noise. Sarah, her mother and her dad were sitting around the kitchen table. They had lit a smelly kerosene lantern because the storm had knocked down a power line.

"That was just the wind," her mother said. She looked frightened by the storm and her father was holding her mother's hand.

"It will calm down by morning," Sarah's father said, trying to be reassuring.

"What if you lose the boat?"

"I have her tied up real good. She won't go anywhere. That old boat wouldn't know where else to go."

"Be serious," Sarah's mother said. She was staring deep into the flame.

"Stop worrying," he said.

"That's easy for you to say," Sarah's mother snapped back.

"There, I heard it again," Sarah said. "It sounded like someone crying."

"It's just your imagination," her mother explained.

"No, it isn't," Sarah insisted. She ran to the back door and threw it open. A torrent of wind and rain rushed into the room. The wind blew out the lamp and they were thrown into total darkness.

"Now what?" Sarah's mother groaned, always expecting the worst.

"Just be calm," her father said. "I'll find the flashlight. "Sarah, close the darned door!"

The door slammed shut and Sarah's father fell over a chair in the dark as he tried to find the flashlight. Outside, the wind howled.

Her father found the flashlight and flicked it on to find little Sarah sitting on the wet floor by the door. In her arms was a little puppy.

"Well, I'll be darned," her father said. "Where'd he come from?"

"I don't know, but he's found us now," Sarah answered. "We're keeping him."

Her father was relighting the old kerosene lantern. "Well, I don't know. Your mother isn't very fond of dogs. Besides, he probably belongs to someone. What do you think, dear?" he asked his wife.

Sarah was so busy hugging the little squirmy puppy that she didn't even look up to see her mother crying and shaking her head up and down. "Yes," she said. "We'll keep him until we find his real home."

Now the storm had picked up even more strength. The waves pounded at the wharf. The wind tore at the wooden shingles on the roof until it set some of them free.

"It's going to be a long night," her father announced.

"This is the best night of my life," Sarah said.

They searched for the puppy's owner, but when no one claimed him, Sarah's mother said they could keep him.

"What do you want to name him, Sarah?" she asked.

Sarah thought long and hard. "I don't know. There are so many good names. You pick one."

"I always liked the name, Jeremiah," her mother said. "I think maybe if you'd had a brother, I might have called him Jeremiah."

"But maybe you should save that name in case I do have a brother."

"No, I don't think that will happen." Her mother looked at her with sad, gentle eyes. "I want you to use the name for the puppy."

The year Sarah found Jeremiah the fishing was good. Sarah's dad went to sea during the fine weather and filled the boat with cod and hake and haddock and flounder. He sold the catch to the fish plant further up the inlet and came home with money in his pockets.

Her dad seemed to like getting up at five-thirty in the morning when it was still dark and going off to sea in his boat alone. "It's good to get back up the inlet before the winds come up," he'd explain. But Sarah's mother worried about him out there by himself. She always expected the worst to happen. Even in the good times.

"Stop your frettin'," he'd say. "I'm very careful." He had a big, wonderful smile on his face.

"Never smile before Christmas," his wife chided him. "You never know what can go wrong. You don't want to tempt fate with all that over-confidence."

But her dad kept smiling anyway.

Chapter Three

These days Sarah often sat in her
room with Jeremiah and read books.
Her favourite book was *Anne of Green
Gables*, which she read over and over
even though her father said it was a
book for older kids. She didn't have
many friends because she lived such a
long way from town. It took a half hour
in their old Chevy pick-up truck to
drive down the muddy gravel road to
her school. Sarah had tried to keep
track of the number of potholes.

"Three thousand and seventy-five."

"What?" her mother asked.

"Three thousand and seventy-five potholes to school and back."

"And next year there'll be four thousand and seventy-five," her mother answered.

Jeremiah would ride in the back of the pick-up and sniff at the air. He looked strong and proud riding back there. When Sarah would come home from school, they would go hiking along the beaches where Sarah would imagine them having all sorts of adventures.

Sometimes they pretended to look for buried treasure. Sometimes they pretended they had been shipwrecked. Other times they would find real sea creatures like starfish and jellyfish stranded on the shore. Sarah would always put them back into the water.

Even though Jeremiah never hurt another animal, he loved to chase spruce grouse, weasels, otters or ducks. Sarah tried to stop him, but Jeremiah had too much wild energy that just had to be released.

That was until one day when he went too close to a porcupine. He was only playing when he ran up to it and nipped at the porcupine's fur which turned out not to be fur at all but hundreds of sharp needles.

Jeremiah howled in pain and began swinging his head back and forth. Sarah ran to him and found his mouth filled with porcupine needles. Sarah thought Jeremiah might die. She didn't know what to do. Jeremiah didn't seem to want to follow her. He was acting crazy from the pain. Sarah tried to pick him up but he was almost as big as she was.

She heard an engine from a boat coming from the inlet and ran to the stony beach. Her father was just rounding Far Enough Island, headed home. Sarah waved and yelled for almost five minutes until her dad was close enough to see her. He pulled his boat in to shore, threw in the anchor and jumped into the shallow water.

"What is it?"

"It's Jeremiah. He chased a porcupine. Now I think he's going to die."

Sarah's father ran into the woods with her and found Jeremiah lying down now. He wasn't moving.

Sarah's father picked him up and carried him to the boat. "Come on, honey," he said to Sarah. "We have to get the boat up the inlet to town before the tide gets too low."

On the boat, Sarah's father roared the engine and they charged toward town.

Sarah knew that her father would never take the boat up the tricky, shallow inlet with the tide dropping unless it was a dire emergency. It was too easy to hit a rock or get stuck on a sand bar. It could wreck the boat. And the boat was his life. Without it he

could not earn enough money for them to live.

"Sit up front and look for logs or rocks or shallow water," he yelled. "Just hold on tight."

Sarah had to lie down on the bow of the boat with both hands braced on the deck. She yelled to her father to go right or left whenever she saw something ahead. The tide was dropping fast and the water was getting more shallow.

Jeremiah lay very still on the deck beside the fish. He was breathing but his eyes looked funny.

"Is he going to die, Daddy?" Sarah asked.

"No," he shouted. "Just keep the look out."

Sarah knew that if they got stuck, they might never get Jeremiah to the vet in time. She watched the water ahead very carefully, shouting when she saw a grassy shallow or a rock ahead.

At the vet's, the woman gave Jeremiah a needle. "This way he won't feel any pain," she said.

Sarah thought the vet meant she was putting him to sleep for good. "No! You can't!" she screamed.

Her father pulled her back and the vet smiled. "He's not going to die." When she pulled out the needle, she took a pair of pliers and began to gently remove the porcupine quills. Sarah counted twenty in all.

"He's a very lucky dog to have two friends like you," the vet said.

Sarah's dad had to phone her mother to come pick them up. The tide was too low to get the boat back down the inlet toward the sea, toward home.

"You could have wrecked the boat," her mother said to them in the truck. Jeremiah was asleep across her dad's lap.

"I couldn't just let him die, could I?" her father answered. Sarah remained quiet.

"Well, it's just a dog," her mother said. "If you lost the boat, then what would we do for money?"

"It's not just a dog," Sarah said, angry now. Her mother didn't understand at all.

Her mother stopped the truck. She turned off the engine and threw the keys at Sarah's father. Then she got out, slammed the door and began walking.

"I'm walking. You drive home, just the two of you. I'm the one who does all the worrying around here. Get on with you."

Sarah's father tried to stop her but it did no good. He lay Jeremiah on the seat and slid over to drive.

"Why is she like that?" Sarah asked.

"It's hard to explain," her father said. "She had it tough when she was growing up. And I think she always hoped I'd be something more than a fisherman."

"What's wrong with being a fisherman?"

"Well, sometimes you have it good and sometimes you have bad times. The sea can be a dangerous place. You know your mother's father drowned."

"But you can swim, right?"

"Sure, I can swim," he said, repeating the lie he'd told so many times he half believed it.

Chapter Four

Just like Sarah's mother had predicted, things did get worse. There were fewer and fewer fish. The weather was stormier and colder in the fall. With less fish and fewer days in the season, the fish plant closed down and there was no place to sell what little catch there was. Her father lost his boat to the bank because he couldn't keep up payments. He took a job at a garage in town fixing cars but he hated working there.

"At least it's money coming in," Sarah's mother would say. "But I know it's going to get worse before it gets better. If it ever does get better."

Sarah didn't like school very much and, now that her father was working in town, she had to hang around the gas station until five o'clock when he got off work so he could drive her home.

She missed her long afternoon walks along the beach with Jeremiah. She hated the garage which always smelled of cigarettes and grease and gasoline. Men and boys stood around and talked tough. Her father was always telling them to use good language when Sarah was around, but they didn't listen. Sometimes they made fun of Sarah's father because he had been a fisherman.

She really missed waking up in the morning and seeing her father's boat way off out to sea toward Far Enough Island. She missed how happy her father had been coming home to the wharf with a boat load of fish.

It was a cold winter and a chilly spring. Even summer wasn't much fun with her father working in town and her mother worrying about the future. In September she was back in school.

"Since you're not fishing any more, we might as well sell the place and move to town," her mother said. "It would be better for Sarah and it would be better for us."

"Jeremiah would hate it in town," Sarah said.

"Then we'd just have to find Jeremiah a new home. He costs us an arm and a leg to feed anyway. And we need to save all the money we can. Hard times might be ahead."

Sarah's father looked down at the floor but didn't say a thing.

The next day he took Sarah to town, but he didn't take her to school. First, they went to the bank and he took out all their savings. Then they drove over to Old Man Fogerty's little run-down wharf on a narrow channel of the inlet.

Old Man Fogerty had been a fisherman for many years. Now he was eighty-five years old. "She's a good boat," he said. "Old, but good. You treat her well, she'll last you a few years."

The boat had a name painted on the side. Fogerty had named her *"Doris."*

The boat was certainly old. But it didn't look so good.

"All she needs is a little paint," her father said. "With a little luck I'll be able to afford better in a couple of years."

Her father handed over the money and he helped Sarah onto the boat.

"What will *she* say?" Sarah asked, thinking about her mother.

"I don't know. I just know I'm fed up with the garage and I don't want to move to town. Now lie down up front there and help me steer out the channel to home before the tide slips."

So Sarah helped guide her dad and his new boat home.

The engine made loud coughing noises. It sputtered and stalled several times but eventually they made it. When they pulled up, Sarah's mother was standing on the wharf with her arms folded and a mean look on her face. When Jeremiah spotted them, he came racing down the boards and launched himself off the wharf before her mother could stop him. He jumped halfway to the boat before splashing down and swimming the rest of the way. Sarah's dad helped him up over the side and, as Jeremiah shook the water off, he sprayed Sarah and her dad until they were soaked.

It was a very funny scene, but Sarah's mother wasn't laughing at all.

Sarah's father worked night and day at fixing up the boat.

"It's too old," Sarah's mother said.

"Fogerty says there's life in her yet."

"I don't trust you out there alone in that old boat. Something could happen."

"Why don't you take Jeremiah along?" Sarah said. "Just for company."

"He'd only get in the way," her father replied. "A dog's not much good on a boat."

"But he likes the water."

Sarah's mother added, "Yes, why not take the dog with you. Get him out from being under foot."

Sarah's father nodded. He didn't mind having a little dog company on board if it gave his wife one less thing to worry about.

It was getting late in the year for a good start but the fish had begun to come back now and there was plenty to catch.

Sarah missed Jeremiah jumping up and licking her in the face every morning but she did get to play with him after school. And she liked the idea of Jeremiah being out there with her father every day, out beyond Far Enough Island. The only problem was that Jeremiah always smelled like fish now so he wasn't allowed to stay in the house any more.

"I knew everything would work out," her father told the family one night at dinner. "The boat is working great. The fish are back. I'm even getting a pretty good price for the catch. I'll have a newer boat soon."

"I think having Jeremiah on the boat brings you good luck," Sarah said. Sarah and her father looked at each other and beamed.

Sarah's mother wasn't convinced. "It's always calmest just before the storm," she said. "Season's not over yet. Just wait."

Then one bright clear morning, the wind switched and a heavy fog pulled up the inlet.

It was a Saturday and Sarah was not in school. Her mother stared out the window and began to wring her hands together. "I hope he gets back in here soon.

"He'll be okay," Sarah said. "He knows the inlet out there. Don't worry."

But her mother worried.

Chapter Five

Her father would have high-tailed it shoreward before the fog but he was having trouble with the engine. The old contraption was giving him problems. Water had gotten mixed in with the gas. He was stalled and drifting, still trying to fix the problem, when the fog pulled in so heavy that he couldn't see a thing. Then the wind stopped and it was dead still.

Jeremiah was nervous, nosing around the boat, wondering why it was quiet and why they weren't moving.

Sarah's father lifted the engine cover and was pouring gasoline down the carburetor. He tried the ignition. It backfired a couple of times. Then suddenly it coughed a long flame out of the mouth of the carburetor, knocking him off balance and back onto the slimy pile of the day's catch. Before he could turn off the ignition, gasoline leaked out of the fuel line and ignited.

Sarah's father grabbed a heavy tarp and threw it across the engine. But it too caught fire. Jeremiah was barking fiercely, as if the fire was a living thing he could fend off.

The fire began to creep out onto the floorboards. It was headed toward the gas tank. Sarah's father tried to jump past it to get to the small cabin to grab a life vest. Just then a violent burst of flame roared up from below the deck, knocking him overboard. In the water, he flailed his arms. He kept telling himself that he *did* know how to swim. He had told that to his wife so often he truly believed it. The water was so cold. It was like sharp knives sticking into his arms and legs. On the boat, Jeremiah continued to bark.

"Here. Jeremiah. Jump!" he yelled.

Jeremiah launched into the water and swam toward him.

Now the entire boat was aflame. Within minutes it would be down. There was no explosion, just the crackle of burning wood.

All too soon, the water was up to the gunwales and the flame diminished to nothing as the boat sank. Still hanging onto Jeremiah to keep himself afloat, Sarah's father swam back to where the boat had gone down, hoping to find a plank, or any piece of wood to hold onto and keep him up. He found a small section of the hull that had been left floating. It wasn't much, but it was enough to keep his head above water.

Around them was a pool of oil, gas and black ash. The fog was now so dense he couldn't see more than ten feet in any direction.

Jeremiah pulled himself up onto a small section of deck that was nearby. At first he began to whine. But then he shook himself and began to bark loudly.

"I'm sorry, Jeremiah," Sarah's father said. "I don't know what good barking will do you. You might as well save your breath."

But Jeremiah went on barking louder and louder. It was like he had gone crazy and couldn't stop himself.

Sarah's father felt so cold and weak from being in the water that he began to lose hope. There was nothing more he could do and he felt helpless and doomed. The dog barked on and on till he wished he could make Jeremiah shut up.

After a long time of hanging onto the wood that kept him afloat, Sarah's father thought he heard a boat engine.

It was far off in the fog but coming closer.

"Keep barking!" he now shouted to Jeremiah, but Jeremiah was floating away from him.

The boat was coming closer. Sarah's father convinced himself he had to move. He let go of the wood and began to swim as best he could toward the engine noise. Then he heard Jeremiah splash into the water and swim up to him. "Over here!" he yelled to whoever was coming to help. But as he did so, his mouth filled with water. He felt himself sinking. He reached out with his hands and there was Jeremiah. He grabbed the collar, pulling the dog under with him, but Jeremiah kicked his legs and kept swimming.

The boat was nearly on top of them.

"Cut the engine, quick!" someone shouted. Arms were reaching down. Sarah's father was pushing down on Jeremiah, struggling to keep himself above water. He knew he was probably drowning the dog, but it was the only thing he could do to keep from sinking altogether.

Then somebody grabbed him. He was being hauled up into a boat. Within seconds, he was flat on the deck and his lungs were heaving, gasping for air.

"Anybody else out here?" a man's voice asked frantically.

"A dog," Sarah's father said. "Jeremiah. Did you get Jeremiah?"

"I didn't see a dog but that's why I came this way. I heard some fool dog barking his head off. But if he was out there he's not around now," the man said.

Sarah's father pulled himself up and looked over the side. There was nothing to see. No Jeremiah, nothing but a thick, ugly fog.

They circled around for twenty minutes but saw and heard nothing.

"He saved my life," Sarah's father said and sank back onto the floor.

Chapter Six

At home, the next day, Sarah's mother said, "I told you things would get worse. I felt it in my bones. We're just a family with bad luck."

"That's not true," Sarah shouted back. "If it wasn't for Jeremiah, Dad wouldn't be here. He wouldn't be alive."

Her dad hung his head down. "That's right. I have to go back out there and look for him. I'll get somebody to loan me a boat."

"Not in this weather, you're not," Sarah's mother insisted.

"I suppose you're right. One swim in the sea is one too many."

"But we need to look for him!" Sarah screamed. "He might be alive."

"He couldn't swim all the way back here," her father said.

"But he might have made it to the island. He could have, you know."

Her father shook his head. "I don't think so. I don't know how close to the island we were. Besides, how could he find it in all that fog?"

"He's gone, Sarah," her mother said. "Now let's just leave it at that."

By the next morning the sun was out. "I'm going to look for him. I've got the use of a boat." Sarah's father had a life jacket on. Just then Sarah burst out of her room. She had one on as well. "I'm going too," she announced.

Her father put an arm around her and gave her a hug. "Sure. We'll both look for him."

Her mother looked furious. "Sure, get both of you drowned now. That's all I need."

Sarah's father walked up to his wife and touched her shoulders. He kissed her on the cheek and whispered something in her ear.

"We'll be careful," Sarah said to her mother. "We won't go past the island. We just have to look once."

They were gone most of the day. Sarah and her father walked all around Far Enough Island and looked everywhere along the beaches. But there was no sign of Jeremiah.

"I'm sorry, honey," her father said.

Sarah tried not to cry but she couldn't help it. "He was my only real friend," she said, and the tears kept coming all the way home.

They had a big dinner but ate in silence. At the end, her father announced he would try to get his job back at the garage.

After that, the weather turned very cold for so early in the year. All the fishermen pulled up their boats weeks before they normally would have. Raging northeast storms pummelled the coast. Then came snow in October. Sleet and ice and snow. Schools were closed. Sarah's father got fired from his garage job when he told his boss that he thought they were overcharging.

Sarah's mother always wore a frown on her face. "We should have just packed up and moved long ago. Now's the time. Let's just get away from here."

But Sarah didn't want to move. She kept remembering those happy, sunny days walking the shoreline with Jeremiah. She still couldn't believe he was gone. Now she sat in her room alone and read *Anne of Green Gables*, pretending she was Anne, not Sarah. But it only helped a little. Some mornings she'd wake up and expect Jeremiah to come bounding into her room, smelling of fish and mud. But she kept reminding herself that if it wasn't for Jeremiah, she wouldn't have a father.

Chapter Seven

It was Christmas morning but things had been so rotten around Sarah's house for so long that she knew this day would be like all the rest. The day was dark and stormy, with sleet and ice pellets falling from the sky.

Only a miracle would make things better. Her parents argued all the time about money and about moving. Sarah would get so tired of it all that she'd scream, "Shut up!" and lock herself in her bedroom.

It had been a strange December. The harbour froze up early and the ice grew thick across the shallows right out into the channel.

"It's a sign of worse things to come," her mother said. "I've never seen anything like it."

They could no longer afford oil for the furnace so her father spent hours every day cutting spruce logs, hauling them home, splitting them, and stoking the stoves.

The ice had crept all the way out the inlet, almost to Far Enough Island. It was the first time that had happened since 1915, Old Man Fogerty said. It was going to be a long, cold, sad winter.

"But today is Christmas," her mother said. "And I'm not going to worry about a thing. Today I want all of us to be happy."

She wasn't very convincing but she tried. She had always said it was the one day she refused to worry about anything. She woke Sarah early in the morning, even before the sun was up, with a peck on the cheek.

"Merry Christmas, Sarah."

But Sarah woke up thinking about Jeremiah and all the other Christmases he had been there. She remembered how he had torn up the wrapping paper to get at his presents — dog bones and leather chew toys. He had been so funny and so cute. And she would never, ever see him again.

Her mother tried singing to Sarah to cheer her up, but it didn't do any good.

The presents were opened. Sarah tried to act surprised and happy but nothing interested her.

Her father tried to be cheerful but he was a poor faker.

By the end of the day, her mother's good humour had worn off and they all sat around tired and depressed.

"This is the worst Christmas of my life," Sarah finally said out loud. "I never want to have another Christmas as long as I live." She sulked off to her room, slammed her door and went to bed.

Chapter Eight

By the day after Christmas, the ice storm had stopped. The sun was shining brightly as Sarah flipped open the shade on her window. All the trees were coated in ice and the inlet was one sheet of pure, clear glass. The wharf glistened like some amazing creation coated in crystal. And off in the distance, Far Enough Island, with all the trees glazed with ice, gleamed like a distant magical kingdom.

Sarah just wanted to keep looking out her window. She didn't want to go down to her family and face all the gloom and worry. If only she could just stare out her window like this forever and see the world as a beautiful, mystical place, everything would be all right.

Just then, off in the far distance, she saw a small, dark speck that caught her attention. Out toward Far Enough Island something was moving on the ice. An otter, she decided. She would get her father's binoculars and watch him.

She slipped quietly out of her bed and into her parents' bedroom. They were still asleep. By the window were the binoculars. She returned with them to her room.

At first she couldn't find the animal again in the glare of ice. But then she spotted it. Maybe it wasn't an otter, after all. It was larger than an otter, for sure. And it had longer legs. It was running. Running toward her.

Her eyes began to tear up. She couldn't focus properly. She wiped her face. Yes, whatever it was, it was running. It kept slipping and falling on the ice. But it was running toward her across the inlet. She closed her eyes and pinched herself to make sure she was awake. She had had dreams like this before. And always when she opened her eyes, she was alone, and the image was gone.

She re-opened her eyes. The pinch had hurt. She was awake. She looked through the binoculars again.

It was him. It was Jeremiah.

The ice stretched from Far Enough Island all the way to her shore. He was on his way home.

Sarah raced downstairs and outside into the bright, cold air.

"Jeremiah!" she yelled, out across the vast expanse of ice.

Then she heard the first bark. It was his unmistakable bark. She started to run toward him, out across the

frozen yard, but she slipped and fell. *Everything* was covered with ice and it was almost impossible to take a step.

Her shout had awakened her father and mother. They were soon beside her, helping her up.

"He was there after all," her father said, his eyes fixed on Jeremiah, still making his difficult way toward them across the ice.

"I don't believe it," Sarah's mother said. She was smiling and wiping tears from her eyes at the same time.

All three of them, still in their night clothes, began a slow, slippery walk across the icy yard toward the inlet, toward Jeremiah. Sarah wanted to run, but her parents held her back. When they reached the wharf, Jeremiah's feet were going every which way as he scratched the ice to make his way home.

Sarah knelt down on the cold, glassy surface and felt the hot, familiar breath of Jeremiah. She let him lick her face and bark loud as a canon right in her ear.

With a lot of slipping and sliding, they all found their way back into the warm kitchen, where Jeremiah was treated to all the leftover Christmas dinner he wanted.

"He had made it to the island," her father said, "and he was too tired or injured for us to find him. When the inlet froze up all the way to the island he came back."

Sarah hugged Jeremiah again and then sat down at the kitchen table with her mother and father. The morning sun made the kitchen bright and warm. Her mother looked at Sarah and there was no worry in her eyes. Her father reached out and touched his wife's hand.

Jeremiah's return had changed everything.

It wouldn't matter if the fish never came back or if the money was tight or if the whole world froze solid. There would always be this moment that would make every one of them smile, any time of the year.

Other Books in this Series

To order, phone toll-free:
1-800-NIMBUS9 (1-800-646-2879)